VLAD
THE WORLD'S
WORST
VAMPIRE

To Albert, who looked fang-tastic in his Vlad costume
for World Book Day
– A.W.

For my talented cousin Elizabeth who never ceases
to impress me!
– K.D.

First American Edition 2020
Kane Miller, A Division of EDC Publishing

First published in Great Britain in 2018 by STRIPES Publishing,
an imprint of the Little Tiger Group.

For information contact:
Kane Miller, A Division of EDC Publishing
PO Box 470663
Tulsa, OK 74147-0663
www.kanemiller.com
www.edcpub.com
www.usbornebooksandmore.com

Library of Congress Control Number: 2019956276

Printed and bound in the United States of America
2 3 4 5 6 7 8 9 10
978-1-68464-165-9

VLAD THE WORLD'S WORST VAMPIRE

Midnight Fright

ANNA WILSON
ILLUSTRATED BY
KATHRYN DURST

Kane Miller
A DIVISION OF EDC PUBLISHING

1

Vlad shivered. He was standing in the graveyard outside Misery Manor with his parents and grandfather by his side. It was a chilly, cloudy night and the sky was as black as a bat's wing. There was not a star in sight – even the moon seemed to have gone into hiding.

Vlad pulled his cape around himself. He hated the graveyard and he hated the dark. He was also nervous. He was waiting for the arrival of his cousin, Lupus Fang, who was coming from Transylvania that very night.

Vlad's parents, Drax and Mortemia, had invited Lupus to stay to show Vlad "how to be a real vampire."

Mother and Father have already decided that he's a much better vampire than me, Vlad thought as he scanned the inky sky for signs of his cousin's arrival. *I don't want to have my lessons with him. He'll make me seem even more of a failure.* He shivered again.

"Whatever is the matter with you?" snapped his mother. "Vampires do not feel the cold!"

"It's not that," said Vlad through chattering fangs. "I d-don't like the dark."

"Well, it's about time you did," Mortemia retorted. "You don't want your cousin Lupus to see you quivering, do you?"

"I don't care if he does," Vlad muttered. "I never wanted him to come anyway."

His father snorted. "If you were better at

your vampire skills then we wouldn't have had to invite him. Although I must admit that your mind control is coming along nicely." He chuckled at the memory of Vlad shrinking his mother to the size of a spider.

The thought of spiders made Vlad shiver all the more. *I bet there are hundreds of them out here*. He felt as though his skin was crawling with them!

Grandpa Gory joined in with Drax's chuckling, as if reading his thoughts. "Mwhaha!" he chortled wheezily. "That was wicked!"

Mortemia glared at the old vampire. Gory immediately turned his laugh into a cough and slunk into the shadows.

"I'd rather you put your skills to better use," said Mortemia bitterly. "You'd better not try shrinking your cousin, either."

Flit the bat flew down from the yew tree in the corner of the graveyard. He landed on Vlad's shoulder. "Don't let them upset you," the little bat whispered. "I'll stick with you."

"Thanks," Vlad said. He didn't know what he would do without Flit. He'd already told the bat all his fears about his cousin coming to stay.

"He can't be good at *everything*," Flit squeaked, flying up and hovering by Vlad's side.

But Lupus's perfect vampire skills were the least of Vlad's worries. Worse than that, Vlad was anxious that his cousin would find out his biggest secret – that he went to human school!

"Here he is!" shouted Drax, startling Vlad out of his thoughts. He pointed toward a dark shape coming through the night sky toward them.

Vlad followed his father's long bony finger. The black thing was moving at top speed. Vlad felt sure it was aiming straight for him! He squealed and dipped behind a tombstone for cover, then peeped around it. The shape was getting closer and closer and seemed to be accompanied by a swirling cloud of other smaller shapes.

"What are all those things flying with him?"

he asked in alarm.

Mortemia tutted. “They’re carrier bats, of course. How else do you think Lupus would be able to bring his luggage?”

“Carrier bats!” cried Grandpa Gory. “Good to see they’re still using them in the old country.”

“Yes,” said Drax. “They may be more modern than us in *some* things, but Transylvanian vampires still use the old-fashioned methods of travel.”

Vlad crept out from behind the tombstone and stared up at the shapes as they came closer. His mother was right – a tight swarm of bats was circling now, each clutching a bag in their claws. In the midst of them was a larger bat.

Vlad couldn’t see very clearly because his night vision was still not as good as it should’ve been. He squinted at the big bat.

It must be Lupus, Vlad thought. *Father said he was big and strong. I wish he would turn around and go back home.*

Vlad screwed his eyes shut. He made himself think about how angry he was. Then he focused on sending Lupus away, using mind control.

He imagined Lupus being surrounded by the carrier bats…

...the bats would swoop him up and turn him around...

...Lupus would be powerless to resist...

...he would be carried back to Transylvania...

Suddenly, Vlad felt the air around him grow even colder. His mind went cloudy. It was as though someone were pushing his thoughts out of his brain, freezing him so that he couldn't move, couldn't think...

Vlad tried to concentrate but it was no use. The cloudiness became heavier and darker, and he himself became colder and colder. He found that he couldn't remember where he was or what he was thinking.

Then...

THWACK!

Something slapped into Vlad, pushing him back into the tombstone. He bumped his head.

"OW!" He struggled to sit up and blinked into the darkness. "What was that?" he cried.

"You should keep your eyes open, buddy," said a voice. "Especially when you're in the flight path of an incoming vampire. Mwhahahahaha!"

Vlad shrieked and ducked back behind the tombstone, while Mortemia burst out laughing.

"Bravo!" Drax applauded. "What a landing. Superfast nosedive!"

"Like a hawk plummeting toward its prey," added Grandpa Gory approvingly.

Vlad peeked back around the stone to get a good look at his cousin. Lupus was the same age as Vlad, but even in the dark it was clear how much taller and stronger he was.

Vlad groaned inwardly. "Thanks, Uncle D.," Lupus said to Drax. "It's great to finally get here."

R.I.P.

Uncle D.? Vlad thought. *Father won't like that nickname.*

But Drax gave Lupus a hearty slap on the shoulder and said, "We've been looking forward to your visit, young devil."

"Did you have a good flight?" Mortemia asked, brushing down Lupus's cape. "You're brave to come all this way on your own."

Drax nodded. "It's a long way from Transylvania."

"In my day, young vampires had to have an adult flying with them," said Grandpa.

"Yeah well, this is the twenty-first century, not the seventeenth," said Lupus with a grin.

Drax chuckled. "That's true!" he said.

Vlad gasped. He was speechless at how his cousin had gotten away with being so cheeky.

Flit gave a disapproving squeak, but Mortemia and Drax didn't notice. They

seemed enchanted by Lupus.

"There was a bit of turbulence on the way over," Lupus told them, "but I just went with the flow. You know what it's like – if you relax you can fly through anything."

Drax looked at Mortemia approvingly. "Just what I always say, isn't it, my evil one?"

"Indeed," said his mother crisply. "In fact, perhaps you can take Vlad on a night flight a bit later, Lupus? You're here to work, after all."

"Sure. I can show Vlad some tricks," Lupus replied carelessly.

Vlad scowled.

Lupus noticed Vlad's expression and his grin faltered. "Maybe some other time. I'm pretty hungry now," he said.

Drax clapped his hands and roared, "Of course! An energetic young vampire like you needs his iron. Let's get you inside."

"Yes," Mortemia said. "Why don't you dismiss your bats, Lupus? They're welcome to stay in the belfry. Flit will show them the way."

The bats began to cluster around Flit.

"Sorry, Vlad!" Flit squeaked. "I'll come and see you later."

Then he flew off to the belfry at the far end of Misery Manor with the carrier bats following.

Vlad watched sorrowfully as his bat friend disappeared into the darkness.

"Mulch will bring the bags," Mortemia was saying. "And Vlad, you can show Lupus your room – you'll be sharing," she explained to Lupus.

"What?" Vlad exclaimed. "Why can't he stay in the West Wing? There are loads of spare coffins there."

"Vladimir!" Drax exploded. "Lupus is one

of the family and will be treated as such. Show him to your room immediately. I've already asked Mulch to move a coffin in for him. Why don't you join us in the dining room for lunch once Lupus has unpacked?"

"Hmm, lunch!" said Grandpa Gory, smacking his lips. "I thought you'd never ask." He began hobbling toward the house with Mortemia and Drax on either side of him.

Vlad eyed Lupus's bags. He'd brought so much luggage! *It looks as though he's planning to stay forever,* he thought.

"Come on then, Lupus," Vlad said gloomily.

He turned and made his way into Misery Manor with Lupus close behind.

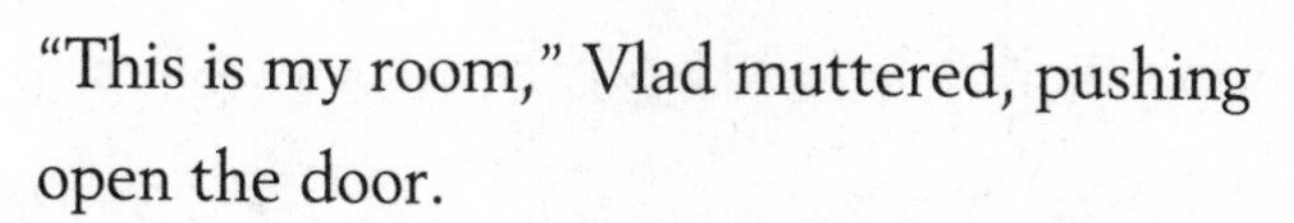

"This is my room," Vlad muttered, pushing open the door.

Lupus said nothing as he walked around, taking a good hard look at everything.

Vlad meanwhile, was taking a good hard look at Lupus! In many ways he looked like a traditional vampire: he had jet-black hair, huge fangs and he wore an expensive-looking black velvet cape lined with red silk.

However, under the cape, Vlad could see clothes that looked distinctly un-vampiric. Curiously, they looked a lot like the clothes

Vlad wore to human school. Lupus had human sneakers on his feet, too – and they flashed when he walked! Vlad felt a mixture of confusion and envy.

Mother and Father would never EVER let me wear shoes as cool as that! he thought.

Lupus peered at the cobweb-covered ceiling. Then his gaze went to the heavy oak chest where Vlad hid his private possessions.

I hope Lupus doesn't go and poke his nose in there, Vlad thought.

If he did, he would discover a stash of books which Vlad had borrowed from the school library. And the book report Vlad had written for his teacher, Miss Lemondrop.

I should have asked Mulch to look after them, he thought.

Mulch was the family butler. He was a good friend to Vlad and knew some of Vlad's secrets – including that he had a best friend called Minxie who was a human!

A cold trickle of horror crept down Vlad's neck as he thought of what might happen if Lupus ever found out about Minxie. It was just too dangerous having his cousin to stay. Lupus suddenly let rip with the evilest laugh Vlad had ever heard.

"MWAHAHAHAAAAAAA!"

"Eek!" Vlad jumped so high he almost

turned into a bat by mistake. He had to reach for his inhaler and take a long puff to recover.

"Sorry," said Lupus, biting back laughter. "It's just – this room…"

"What's wrong with it?" Vlad asked.

"It's so old-fashioned!" Lupus exclaimed. He pointed to the coffins. "They're *so* last century. In Transylvania we sleep in four-poster beds with duvets and pillows. I should've known it would be different here," he added with a chuckle. "Your parents insisted on sleeping in coffins when they came to my house. It's so dusty here, too! No wonder you have to use an inhaler," Lupus went on. "Our family doctor, Dr. Sawitov, says 'if you vacuum each day you keep asthma away.'"

"Vacuum?" said Vlad, looking puzzled.

Lupus gaped at his cousin. "You don't

know what a *vacuum* is? I'm guessing you don't know what a TV is either?" he added. "Or a computer?"

Vlad bristled. "Actually, I *do* know what a computer is – oh!" He clapped his hand to his mouth as he realized what he'd said. The only reason he knew about computers was because of human school – but he couldn't tell Lupus that!

Lupus narrowed his eyes. "You were saying…?" he asked.

Before Vlad could think what to say, two black shapes zipped in through the bedroom door and flew around the room in circles, chasing each other. One of them was Flit.

"Eek! Eek!" the bat shrieked. "Get it off me!"

Vlad scurried behind his coffin and crouched low. "Flit!" he shouted out in bat language. "What's going on?"

Flit plummeted toward Vlad. “It’s a big black bird!” he squeaked. “Help, hide me!”

The bird swooped down, making straight for Flit. Vlad grabbed the little bat and then dived into his coffin and under the covers. He lay there, clutching poor Flit, the two of them quivering with fright.

"Get it out of here!" came Vlad's muffled voice from under his bedspread.

"Mwahahahahaa!" Lupus guffawed.

"You two are such scaredy-bats. It's only Claw," he said.

The large bird came to settle on Lupus's arm.

"Wow, you English vampires are strange. Have you never seen a raven before?" Lupus asked.

Vlad poked his head out from under the covers. "A RAVEN?" he repeated. "IN MY ROOM?"

"It's my room too now, and where I go, Claw goes," Lupus said stubbornly.

"Caw-caw! I'm not staying in the belfry with those weird bats," croaked Claw.

"*Weird?*" squeaked Flit. "I'll show you who's weird." He performed a loop-the-loop and spun around Claw's head until the bird's eyes were rolling in their sockets.

"Stop it!" Claw cried. "You're making me dizzy."

"You stop chasing me, then," said Flit.

"Yeah, leave my bat alone," said Vlad. He felt anger boil up inside him. He wished more than ever that he could make Lupus and the horrible raven disappear.

He closed his eyes and imagined them being sucked outside by a gust of wind...

...out into the corridor and up, up into the Black Tower...

But then the cold feeling that Vlad had had in the graveyard took hold of him again...

...his thoughts became dark and cloudy...

...and he couldn't think of anything at all!

He opened his eyes and shook his head to get rid of the horrible blackness.

"I'm off!" squeaked Flit, whizzing up from under the covers and out through the crack in the door.

"Flit, come back!" Vlad cried. But the bat had already gone. "What happened...?" Vlad

asked, turning to Lupus.

Vlad's cousin looked strange. He was staring hard at Vlad, his expression fierce. Claw was sitting on his shoulder, cackling quietly.

"What are you doing?" Vlad asked, puzzled.

All at once Lupus's stern frown relaxed and he gave one of his maddeningly cheeky grins. "Chill, buddy!" he said. "You'll have to work harder on your mind control. You're far too easy to block." He winked. "You need to do it without getting all stressy. It's like flying – the more you relax, the easier it is."

Vlad snapped with irritation. "Why don't you just go back to—" he began.

STOMP-STOMP-STOMP.

Vlad stopped. He recognized that sound…

Claw shot up to the rafters while Lupus looked inquisitively toward the door. Someone or something was pushing it open

v e r y, v e r y s l o w l y…

"May I come in?" said a deep and gloomy voice.

"Mulch!" cried Vlad, rushing to greet the huge lumbering butler. At last! Someone who was on his side.

The butler was carrying every single one of Lupus's bags in his massive muscly arms. He came into the room and dropped them onto the floor by Lupus's coffin.

"You're Master Fang, I assume?" Mulch asked.

"Yeah," said Lupus, flicking his long hair out of his eyes.

Mulch bowed and turned to Vlad. "Everything all right, Master Impaler?" he asked.

Vlad took a deep breath. He decided that he needed to tell a little fib to get rid of Lupus. Surely Mulch would help him, as he had before now?

"Lupus doesn't want to share my room," Vlad said, speaking quickly. "There's not really enough space—"

"Vlad?" Mortemia's shrill voice echoed along the corridor.

Mulch held up his hand. "Sorry, Master," he said. "The Countess has given her orders and I must obey."

With that, he lumbered out, just as

Mortemia appeared in the doorway. She was carrying a tray with a jug of dark-red liquid and two tall glasses.

"I thought you two were coming to lunch?" she said, glowering at Vlad and Lupus. "Mulch laid the table ages ago. Your lovely warm blood is getting cold. We must get on with lessons – you can drink your meal in here."

She poured two glasses of blood.

"*What?*" Lupus cried. "You guys don't *still* drink blood, do you? This gets better and better!"

Vlad was pleased to see that his mother looked insulted. "Yes, Lupus," she said carefully. "We *do* still drink blood. Drax and I believe it's important to uphold the traditional vampiric ways of life."

Lupus quickly put on a serious face and nodded. "Yeah, I totally get that," he said, taking a glass.

Vlad watched in astonishment as his cousin swallowed the pint of blood down in one long glug.

"Mmm," said Lupus, wiping his mouth on the back of his sleeve. "I'd forgotten how *delicious* traditional vampire food is. Can I have some more, Auntie Morty?"

Mortemia winced slightly at the nickname,

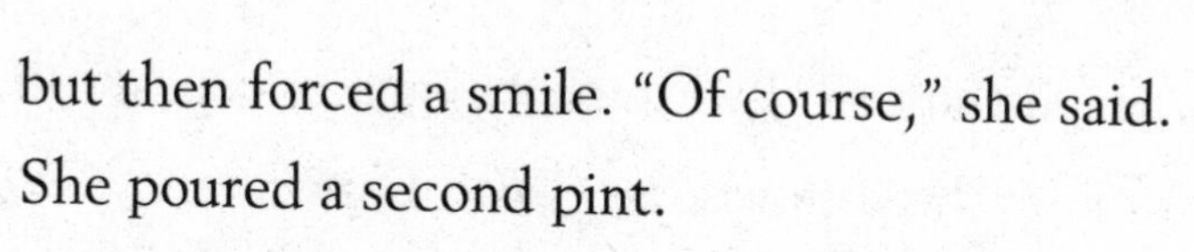

but then forced a smile. "Of course," she said. She poured a second pint.

Lupus glugged it down in one again.

"Devilishly good!" he said. "Just one more?"

Vlad watched miserably as his cousin knocked back a THIRD pint of blood while Mortemia looked on approvingly.

Lupus finished and gave a loud burp. "Shall we go flying now?" he asked.

Vlad held his breath. Surely his mother would tell Lupus off for such bad manners?

But she simply said, "Yes, Lupus. You can show Vlad some of the basic maneuvers he needs to pass his Bat License."

"No problem, Auntie Morty," Lupus replied. He flashed his fangs at her in a dazzling smile.

Mortemia turned to Vlad. "It's about time you got your Bat License, Vladimir, and if you don't learn the maneuvers, you're bound

to fail the test. I've set up an agility course among the tombstones. With Lupus here to show you how, I am sure you'll learn in no time."

Vlad felt his heart flutter. He didn't want to go back into the dark graveyard. And he didn't want to practice maneuvers and skills for his Bat License all night either. If he didn't manage to get to bed early he would never be able to wake up in time to get to school!

He didn't have a chance to protest, however. With every minute that passed, it was becoming clearer to Vlad that his mother was not interested in anything he had to say while Lupus was here.

The rest of the night passed miserably for Vlad. He watched as Lupus did everything effortlessly. Vlad still had to concentrate very

hard to change into a bat by thinking *Batwings – Air – Travel,* as Flit had taught him, whereas Lupus seemed to PING! into bat shape as though someone had flicked a switch in his brain. He performed all the tasks that Mortemia had set with the greatest of ease.

Drax and Grandpa Gory were called to watch. They cheered at everything Lupus did and they groaned whenever Vlad crashed into anything – which was often.

I'm never going to be the vampire my parents want me to be, Vlad thought as he dragged himself, battered and bruised, back to his coffin at daybreak.

As he fell asleep his last thought was that he needed to see Minxie and Miss Lemondrop more than ever before!

Vlad woke to the feeling of something gently tickling his ear.

"URGH!" He shot out of his coffin, brushing frantically at whatever it was, thinking it must be a spider.

"Shhh! It's only me!" said Flit, who was hovering in front of Vlad's face. "It's time for school. Lupus is sound asleep, but I don't know about Claw, so you must be quiet. I'm not even sure where Claw is," Flit added. He flicked his ears nervously.

"SNOOOOOOAAAARRRRRGH!"

Vlad jumped. "What was that?"

Flit giggled. "It was *him*!" he squeaked. He pointed at the other coffin in the room.

Vlad saw a large lump under the bedclothes, which was, of course, Lupus.

"Wow, his snores are worse than Grandpa's!" Vlad whispered.

Flit nodded. "At least we know he's fast asleep," he said. "Come on, let's get you ready for school."

Vlad stood on the edge of his coffin and thought *B – A – T.* Then, POOF! He was a bat. He followed Flit down the dark and dusty corridors of Misery Manor.

"Do you think I'll ever be as good at flying as Lupus is?" he squeaked to Flit as they flew out of the front door.

"Of course," said Flit. "You just need more practice. Now hurry!"

Vlad flew into the sunlit graveyard and

thought *Vampire – Land – Air – Down* as he transformed back to his normal self. Then he went to the yew tree where he hid his school uniform and changed into it quickly. Once more he thought *B – A – T* and flew up into the air next to Flit.

"I hope Claw hasn't seen us," he said, looking at the towers of Misery Manor.

"Don't you worry about the raven," said Flit. "She's *my* problem. Unfortunately," he added with feeling.

"I'm sorry," said Vlad. "I wish you could come to school with me."

"It's all right. I must stay here in any case – you need me to keep an eye on Lupus."

Vlad nodded glumly. "I hope he doesn't wake up. If there's any trouble, go and find Mulch," he said. "He'll know what to do."

Vlad arrived at school just as all the other children were running in through the gates to the playground. He whizzed to the bike shed so that he could secretly transform, then he ran to find Minxie. She was waiting for him by the hopscotch area. Her face lit up when she saw him.

"So?" she asked, running over to him. "What's he like?"

Minxie already knew that Vlad's cousin was coming to stay. She also knew that Vlad's parents had been on a trip to Transylvania to see if it would be a good idea for Vlad to go there too one day. She thought the whole thing was very exciting and didn't understand why Vlad was so down in the dumps about it.

"I'll tell you later," said Vlad grumpily. He had come to school to get away from his cousin. "Can we play hopscotch? I don't want to talk about Lupus."

"Why not? I would LOVE it if my cousin were a vampire the same age as me," Minxie chattered on.

"Don't say that!" said Vlad, looking around. "Boz might hear you."

Boz was the naughtiest boy in the school

and he had taken a dislike to Vlad. In fact, Boz was convinced there was "something strange" about him, so he had followed Vlad home the week before to try and find out what that "something" might be… Luckily Mulch had come along, which had given the boy a huge fright!

Minxie made a face. "You don't need to worry about Boz. He still thinks you're an orphan. Remember how scared he was when Mulch picked him up and took him outside?"

Vlad was not convinced. "Well, ye-es," he said, "but he still hates me – and he said he'd tell the school where I lived."

"You could always use your mind control to stop him," said Minxie.

"It's not that easy—" Vlad began.

"Never mind," Minxie cut in. "Tell me about Lupus!" she pleaded. "You're so lucky. I don't even have a *normal* cousin let alone a

you-know-what cousin."

"Of course you don't," Vlad said. "You have to *be* one yourself to be related to one." He was getting irritated – why couldn't Minxie understand how annoying it was having Lupus to stay?

Minxie looked concerned suddenly. "He's not a bully, is he? Has he been horrible to you?"

"Not exactly," said Vlad. "He was rude about my bedroom, though."

"What?" Minxie exclaimed. "But it's the coolest room in the entire universe! What's his problem?"

"He said it was old-fashioned and dusty," Vlad muttered.

"Well, yeah…" Minxie said, "but isn't that the whole point?" She paused and frowned. "Are you sure he's a real *you-know-what*?"

"Oh, he's a real one, all right," said

Vlad in a low voice. "He can laugh the worst laugh you've ever heard, his bat-flying skills are even better than Father's and he drank THREE PINTS of blood last night. Mother and Father think he's the best. Especially Father," he finished glumly.

"Oh," said Minxie. She chewed her lip. "Never mind. At least you can come here to get away from him. And the school play auditions start today, don't forget!" she added. "I've seen the list – we're doing ours tomorrow after school."

Vlad let his face fall into his hands. "The auditions!" he said.

"What's the matter?" asked Minxie. She put her hands on her hips. "You're not going to pull out, are you?"

Vlad looked up at her, his face a picture of misery.

"I haven't had a chance to think about our routine," he complained. "I spent all of Saturday night doing lessons with Mother, then Lupus arrived and we spent hours practicing for my Bat License."

"OK! OK! STOP!" said Minxie. She held up one hand and pretended she was a police officer. "Just s l o o o o w down, mister!"

Vlad took a deep, wheezy breath. He couldn't help smiling at Minxie. She was funny when she put on different voices.

"Sorry," he said. He reached into his pocket for his inhaler and took a puff.

"That's better," said Minxie as he calmed down. "You worry too much. We can practice our routine here at break and lunch. Or..." Her eyes lit up.

"Or what?" Vlad asked cautiously.

"Or I could come back to your house after school and we could practice in the

kitchen while your cousin is still asleep. Mulch wouldn't mind, would he? And then, when Lupus wakes up, I would get to meet him and if he's being mean to you I could sort him out." Minxie fixed Vlad with a particularly mischievous look.

Vlad was horrified. "You can't!" he exclaimed. "Mulch is one thing – I know that *he* doesn't mind you and me being friends. But what if Lupus tells Grandpa Gory? Or Mother and Father? I'll be locked in the Black Tower and never see you again."

"It can't be *that* bad," said Minxie. But she looked worried.

"It's worse!" Vlad cried.

Minxie put her hand on Vlad's shoulder. "You know, if your parents really are that mean, you should tell a teacher about it."

"His parents aren't mean!" said a voice.

Vlad yelped in surprise.

Minxie turned to face the speaker and said sternly, "You shouldn't sneak up on people like that – especially when they're having a PRIVATE conversation."

Vlad was pointing at the speaker with one finger. "You – you – *you*!" he spluttered. "*How did you get here?*"

"On my scooter," said the stranger.

Minxie looked at Vlad, puzzled. Then she looked back at the stranger who was grinning widely. "Wow!" she breathed. "You have the same teeth."

"That's impossible," said Lupus, for of course that's who it was. "We'd have to share a mouth. Mwahahahaha!"

Minxie squealed with glee. "Two vampires in my school!" she cried.

Vlad found his voice at last. "Shh!" he hissed, looking around the playground. "Don't say that!"

Lupus was the one looking puzzled now. "Why shouldn't she?" he asked. "It's true. I am a vampire."

"Shh!" Vlad hissed. "If you go around telling everyone, we'll get kicked out – or worse."

"But I don't understand," said Lupus. He looked around at the children in the playground. "What do you think will happen to you if people find out?"

"Duh!" Vlad said. "Humans hate vampires! Don't you even know that?"

Lupus gave a fang-tastic grin. "Mwahaha!" he roared. "No, they don't! This is another one of those old-fashioned things your parents have told you, isn't it?"

"It is *not*!" said Vlad.

"It must be – listen, in Transylvania, vampires have human friends all the time. Two of my best friends at school are humans," he finished proudly.

"Cool!" said Minxie.

"I don't believe you," said Vlad.

"You'll just have to come to Transylvania to see for yourself," said Lupus, his hands on his hips. "But I forgot – you need to get your Bat License first, don't you?" he teased.

In spite of her fascination with Lupus, Minxie didn't like seeing him talk to Vlad that way. She glared at him. "Hey, you can't be mean to Vlad. He's my friend."

Lupus didn't seem bothered at all. He

merely winked at Minxie, then stepped onto his scooter and pushed away with his foot. Then he jumped, still on the scooter, and flipped around in the air. He did a loop-the-loop and made a perfect landing. Then he sped toward a bench, jumped onto it and scooted across and off the other side.

A small crowd was gathering around Lupus now. The children were oohing and aahing, their eyes wide with amazement at his tricks. Boz had joined them. He seemed reluctantly impressed, too.

Vlad groaned inwardly. *Trust Lupus to be great at human skills as well,* he thought.

"It's like he can actually fly!" gasped Leisha, one of the girls in Vlad's class.

"Have you seen his sneakers?" said Adam, his eyes wide with envy.

"Hey, who are you?" Ravi called out to Lupus. "Are you a friend of Vlad's?"

Vlad was shaking his head at his cousin, trying to warn him not to say anything.

Lupus ignored him, however. “I’m Vlad’s cousin, Lupus Fang.” He grinned, showing his magnificently white and pointy teeth.

“Makes sense,” said Boz with a nasty laugh. “Freaky teeth must run in your family.”

Vlad felt his blood run cold. He closed his eyes and waited for everyone to realize what the pointy teeth meant. *Lupus is obviously a vampire*, he thought. *His fangs are so huge! They’re going to work out that I am a vampire too…*

But no one did.

Instead Vlad heard Lupus say to Boz, “What, you mean like big noses run in your family? Mwhahaha! Noses – run – get it?” He roared with laughter and the crowd joined in.

Vlad opened his eyes. He knew he should feel relieved that no one had found out his secret, but instead he felt cross. Lupus was

stealing the show here, too.

The children clustered around Lupus, asking him excited questions and begging him to show them more tricks on his scooter.

There wasn't time, however, because the bell had rung and Mr. Bendigo, the teacher on duty, was calling the children to line up for attendance.

"You'll have to go now," Vlad told Lupus in a low voice.

"Hey, what about lessons—" Lupus began.

"You're not coming to lessons," said Vlad. Then he turned his back on his cousin and went to line up with his friends.

After attendance, Vlad and his classmates followed Miss Lemondrop inside.

As they went through the door to Badger Class, Vlad felt a tap on his shoulder.

"Can I sit with you?"

Vlad whipped around. "Lupus!" he hissed. "What are you doing? I said you couldn't come to class with me."

Lupus tried to look innocent. "But I thought that's exactly what Auntie Morty wanted me to do – have lessons with you," he replied.

Vlad wasn't fooled. "You know she meant VAMPIRE lessons," he whispered.

"You shouldn't have made such a racket when you left this morning, if you didn't want me to follow you," said Lupus. "You woke me up."

"You were spying on me, more like!" Vlad said. "Go away, you can't sit with me. I sit next to Minxie."

"Vlad!" Miss Lemondrop called out from her desk. "Come and sit down, dear."

Vlad turned away from Lupus and walked in, doing his best to pretend that his cousin wasn't with him. Lupus, however, clung to him like a bat hanging from a branch.

Miss Lemondrop looked puzzled.

"Who is this?" she asked Vlad, glancing from him to his cousin.

"Good morning, madam," said Lupus. He bowed low, flicking his cape out behind him.

"My name is Lupus Fang. I am Vlad's cousin and I've come to stay."

Minxie slid into her seat and glared at Lupus.

Miss Lemondrop didn't exactly look pleased either. "I see," she said slowly.

Vlad felt his stomach turn to ice. He could already tell that Lupus had no idea how to behave in front of humans. How was he

going to stop Lupus from saying anything to Miss Lemondrop about being a vampire?

He was too panicky to use mind control. *If only I could do it like Lupus* – without *getting angry*, he thought.

"Vlad, you can't bring your cousin to school without permission," Miss Lemondrop was saying firmly. "You boys should go and see Mrs. Viola. As principal, she'll know what to do about this situation. And hang your cape up on the pegs on the way out, please," she added to Lupus.

The other pupils had begun whispering among themselves.

Vlad wasn't listening to them, though. He was trying hard to think angry thoughts so that he could stop Miss Lemondrop from talking.

"Vlad, did you hear what I said?" Miss Lemondrop asked. "I'm going to have to

speak to your parents about this."

Lupus cut in. "You'll never get to meet my aunt and uncle, miss. They're far too traditional. They don't like going out in the day, you see. My parents have been trying to tell them for years that the sun won't burn them if— Ouch! Why did you kick me, Vlad?" Lupus turned to his cousin. He rubbed his leg. "That hurt!"

Everyone was looking at the two vampires now. Minxie was mouthing something earnestly to Vlad, but he was busy thinking hard of how to get rid of Lupus.

If only Mulch were here, he thought.

He imagined his cousin being picked up by

Mulch, just as Mulch had picked up Boz…

…Mulch would carry Lupus outside and across the playground and…

But before he could get any further, a strange coldness and darkness overcame Vlad as it had before. His mind control was being blocked – and there was only one person who could do that!

Vlad's thoughts vanished into the darkness. He opened his eyes and glared at Lupus. His cousin was staring hard at Miss Lemondrop, however.

"Well?" the teacher was saying. "Why did you kick your cousin, Vlad? That's not like you."

Vlad stammered and stuttered with fury. How could Lupus do this to him?

Miss Lemondrop began tapping her foot. She was about to speak again, but then something strange happened to her face.

She opened and closed her mouth, but no words came out...

...her angry frown turned into an expression of puzzlement...

...she put a hand to her forehead and staggered slightly.

"Oh! Miss Lemondrop!" cried Minxie, rushing to her side. "Are you all right?"

An anxious murmur went around the room.

"I – er ... um," said Miss Lemondrop faintly. She removed her huge glasses and peered at them as though she wasn't sure what they were for. Then she put them back on and seemed to see Minxie as though for the first time that day. "Ah, good morning, Malika," she said brightly. "My brain's a bit fuzzy this morning. What was I saying?"

Vlad heard a quiet snigger from Lupus.

He must have used mind control! Vlad thought. He knew he should be grateful, but he

couldn't help worrying about what Lupus might do next. At least Miss Lemondrop seemed to have forgotten all about sending Vlad and Lupus to see Mrs. Viola.

She was smiling at Vlad now.

"So, you were saying, Vlad, that your cousin is staying with you?"

"Ye-es," Vlad said uneasily.

"I've come to find out about life in England," said Lupus. "Then Vlad will come and spend some time with my family in Transylvania."

"A cultural exchange – how lovely!" cried Miss Lemondrop, clasping her hands together. "It's just what this school needs. Perhaps we could all come and visit you next year, Lupus?"

Lupus beamed. "That'd be great," he said. "I'm sure my teachers would like to welcome you."

"I'm not coming. Not if they all look like you," said Boz.

"Boswell!" Miss Lemondrop exclaimed. "That is no way to talk to a visitor."

Lupus didn't seem bothered. "You'd love it, Boz," he said. "There's nothing to be afraid of. We don't *bite* – not these days! Mwhahaha!" he added, showing off his fangs.

The class erupted into giggles – all except Vlad and Minxie, who exchanged anxious glances.

"That's enough, everyone," said the teacher, holding up her hands. She called for silence in her usual way. "One... two...three! That's better." Then, looking at Vlad, she went on, "I can see that Lupus shares your family gift for good humor, Vlad – and what an impressive laugh! Perhaps you'd like to get

involved with our school show while you're here, Lupus? The auditions begin after school today. I'm sure Mr. Bendigo can find something for you to do."

Lupus's grin grew broader than ever. "That'd be WICKED!" he said.

Miss Lemondrop beamed. "All right, we must get on with our lessons. I want you to read your book reports aloud, please. Leisha, you can go first. Lupus, take the desk next to Boswell as Chitra is away today."

"Cool!" said Lupus, and he bounded over to the empty desk at the back of the classroom.

Vlad's heart felt as though it had plummeted into his shoes.

Not the show! Acting's the one thing I'm really good at, he thought miserably. *And now Lupus is going to ruin that, too.*

Vlad didn't enjoy the morning at all. Lupus was getting so much attention! Everyone thought he was funny, and he knew the answers in every lesson.

But what worried Vlad most was that Lupus seemed to have forgotten that he needed to keep quiet about being a vampire. In story writing, Lupus wrote a whole page about life as a vampire in Transylvania. Then Miss Lemondrop read his work out loud!

"'Vampires in England are very different from at home,'" Miss Lemondrop read. "'For

example, my aunt and uncle believe that vampires and humans can't be friends. I'm going to prove them wrong when I tell them what a fantastic day I've had today at this school!'"

There was a pause.

Vlad didn't dare look up.

How could Lupus have done this? Vlad thought. *We'll be chased out of the building for sure! I'll never be able to come here again. I'll have to spend the rest of my life shut away at Misery Manor.*

Poor Vlad squeezed his eyes shut and tried to focus on mind control. If he concentrated, perhaps he could get everyone, including the teacher, to forget what they'd heard...

Suddenly Miss Lemondrop clapped her hands and the whole class joined in. They were giving Lupus a round of applause!

Vlad opened his eyes. Had his mind

control worked after all?

"What an incredible story, Lupus!" said Miss Lemondrop.

Vlad glanced back at his cousin. Lupus looked confused.

"Er, thanks, miss," he said, "but it's not a story—"

"Such a colorful description of the house!" Miss Lemondrop went on. "'Misery Manor' – a *lovely* spooky name," she added. She handed the story back to him. "Well, class, we can all learn from Lupus's writing," she said. "You must come up with a story for homework that is as exciting as his."

Vlad frowned at Lupus, but his cousin just shrugged. It looked as though Lupus had gotten away with it. *At least our secret is still safe,* Vlad thought.

For now.

At break time, Vlad avoided the playground. He didn't want to watch his cousin do tricks on his scooter to an adoring crowd. And he didn't want to hear him tell jokes or tall stories either.

Vlad sneaked off to the library instead and found himself a new *Secret Six* adventure. Then he sat on a beanbag in a corner and began reading.

Minxie came in a little later. "There you are!" she said. "You didn't come and get your snack." She checked that the librarian wasn't looking and handed Vlad some pieces of apple.

"Not hungry," said Vlad, pushing Minxie's hand away.

Minxie sighed and shoved the apple into her skirt pocket. "Don't let Loopy Lupus upset you," she said, sitting down. "At least Miss Lemondrop didn't think his story was real."

"Loopy Lupus," said Vlad. He couldn't help grinning. "That's a good name." Then his face fell again. "Not that I could call him that. He'd probably use mind control to turn me into a worm or something in revenge."

"Forget about him! He's not staying forever," said Minxie. "Anyway, we've got the auditions to think about. Shall we

practice now?"

Vlad huffed. "What's the point?"

Minxie lost her patience. "I'll tell you what the point is, buster!" She leaped to her feet and grabbed Vlad's hand, pulling him up. "You and I are going to get the main parts in the show – we're going to be Hansel and Gretel!"

Luckily for Vlad, the bell rang before he could protest.

Minxie let out an exasperated noise and released his hand. "We've wasted break time now!" she said.

"I have to check my book out," Vlad said, hurrying over to the librarian.

Minxie followed him. "I'm not going to let you give up, Vlad," she said between gritted teeth. "We are going to get those parts *and* we're going to show Lupus what a star you are."

Vlad didn't feel like a star as he slunk back into class. *If anything,* he thought, *it was Lupus who was the star right now*. Vlad's cousin had come in from the playground surrounded

by excited children. It was clear that he had already become the most popular person in the class.

If he auditions for the show, there is no way *I will get the main part,* Vlad thought.

"Cheer up, Vlad," said Miss Lemondrop, seeing his sad face. "I've got some very exciting news for everyone..." She had a twinkle in her eye.

Everyone sat to attention, waiting for the announcement.

"I've just been talking to Mrs. Viola. She's suggested that I take Badger Class on a special camping trip this Friday! We're going to Tangle Wood where we'll learn some forest-school skills," she said.

A gasp went around the room and people immediately began chattering, their eyes shining. Vlad's heart leaped! This was exactly the sort of thing that they did in the book

he'd gotten from the school library – *The Secret Six Build a Den*.

Miss Lemondrop called for silence and held up a piece of paper. "Please take this letter home to your parents," she said. "I need their permission to let you stay out overnight."

Vlad's excitement vanished in an instant. *Overnight?* he thought, his stomach tightening. *There's no way I can sneak away at night!*

What with Lupus staying, the auditions for the show and now this camping trip, living a double life was becoming far, far too complicated for the poor little vampire.

"What's up, Vlad?" Minxie asked, as the children went out onto the playground at the end of the day. "Aren't you excited about the camping trip?"

Vlad shook his head miserably.

"He's afraid of the dark," said Lupus with a chuckle. "Don't worry, Vlad. I'll be there to protect you. Mwhahaha!"

"No, you won't," said Vlad grimly.

"Why not?" Lupus asked.

"Because we can't go!" Vlad cried. He stopped walking and turned to face Lupus. "You just don't get it, do you? Things might be different in Transylvania, but here I have to spend every night doing lessons with my mother and I'm supposed to be asleep in the day. It's hard enough to keep school a secret! How do you think I'm going to be able to sneak out of the house at *night* to go camping?"

Lupus looked at him, wide-eyed. "Whoa, slow down, buddy!" he said. "You really need to learn to relax. I'll help you get away from Auntie Morty, don't worry."

Vlad scowled. "Like you've 'helped' me

today by writing all that stuff about being a vampire in story writing?" he said.

"Yeah, that was awful!" said Minxie, putting her hands on her hips.

"So-rry," said Lupus, making a face. "But I controlled the teacher's mind to stop her asking questions about why I was at school, didn't I?" he said.

Vlad glared at his cousin. *He looks so pleased with himself*, he thought.

"Yeah, how did you do that?" Minxie asked, narrowing her eyes.

"The same way he does everything!" said Vlad crossly. "By being the best – the best at flying, the best at doing tricks on his scooter, the best at writing, the best at making people laugh—"

"STOP!" said Minxie.

The two cousins stared at her. "It's not true that Lupus is the best at making people laugh,"

Minxie said. "YOU are, Vlad. *That's* why you're going to be Hansel in the school show."

Vlad gave an uncertain smile in return. *At least Minxie's on my side,* he thought.

"Come on," he said to his cousin. "We'd better turn into bats so that we can get back quicker. We need to get some sleep before our flying practice with Mother. You can leave your scooter in the bike shed."

"Bye, then," said Minxie with a grin. "And remember to practice your audition piece, too, Vlad!"

"I'll make sure he does," said Lupus with a wink.

The two vampires checked that no one was watching, then they waved goodbye and raced off to the bike shed together.

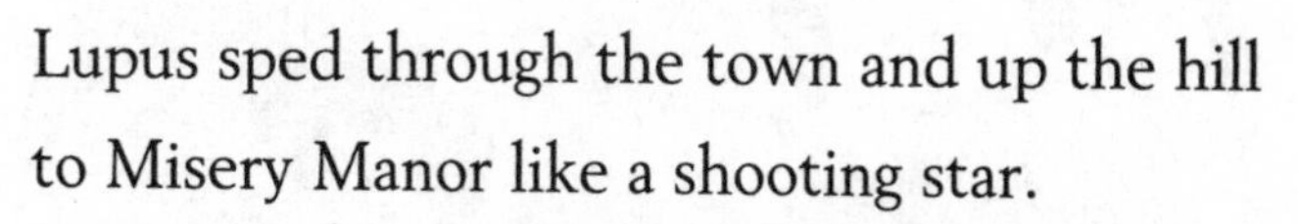

Lupus sped through the town and up the hill to Misery Manor like a shooting star.

Vlad lagged behind. By the time he reached the graveyard, he was completely out of breath and made a terrible landing. He crashed into the yew tree, then fell to the ground in a heap. He was wheezing badly as he transformed into his vampire shape.

"Why do you have to fly so fast, Lupus?" Vlad grumbled, reaching for his inhaler.

"Because it's fun!" Lupus grinned. "Hey, d'you think we can get a snack? I'm starving."

Vlad hesitated. Should he take him down to Mulch's kitchen? He had gone there for tasty snacks himself while his parents were in Transylvania.

Then Vlad thought of how Lupus had gotten all the attention at school. What if Mulch ended up liking Lupus more than him? Vlad wasn't sure he could handle that.

"Come on," Lupus pleaded. "That blood your mom gave me last night was disgusting," he said, screwing his face up.

"But you drank THREE PINTS!" Vlad exclaimed.

"Only to be polite," Lupus said. "Isn't there something we can eat?" He looked suddenly desperate.

Vlad found himself feeling sorry for his cousin. "All right, I'll take you to Mulch's kitchen," he said. "He sometimes gives me nice food. But you mustn't tell Mother or Father,"

he added, giving his cousin a fierce look.

"I won't," Lupus promised in earnest. "Cross my heart and hope to die."

"You don't have to be *that* serious," said Vlad with a frown.

Lupus laughed. "It's just a way of saying I really REALLY promise!" he said. "Come on. My stomach's rumbling."

Vlad took the lead as the two vampires entered Misery Manor. They crept along the dark hallway and down the cold damp stairs to the basement where Mulch worked.

The butler was fast asleep in his armchair by the stove. He stirred and opened one eye when the cousins came in.

"Good afternoon, young devils," he boomed. "I thought you might come looking for something tasty." He gave a huge grin, showing his massive tombstone-like teeth. "There are some cookies on the table and

some hot chocolate in a pan on the stove. Help yourselves."

"Thanks, Mulch," said Vlad.

"Wicked!" said Lupus, his eyes widening.

The cousins took a cookie each and poured themselves a hot drink, then they sat down at the table.

"This is more like it!" Lupus said, running his tongue over his fangs. "So much better than that disgusting blood." He drained his mug of hot chocolate and poured himself another.

Mulch arched one huge furry eyebrow but said nothing.

Vlad was still puzzled. "I don't get why you would drink it if you hate it so much," he said to Lupus.

"If I behave like a good vampire, I'm more likely to get Auntie to be nice to me," Lupus explained.

"That's the most sensible thing I've heard you say since you arrived, Master Fang," said Mulch.

"Too right," said Lupus. "Vlad – I bet if you tried harder at your vampire skills, Auntie Morty wouldn't be so strict with you."

"But that's the problem," said Vlad. "I can try as hard as I like but I'll never be as good as you."

"Rubbish," Lupus scoffed. "You're brave – that's the most important part of being a vampire."

"I'm not brave," said Vlad, frowning.

"Of course you are!" said Lupus. "You'd

have to be brave to creep out of Misery Manor and go to school. If you can do that, you can do anything."

"Oh," said Vlad. He paused. "I'd never thought about it like that," he said.

"He's right," said Mulch.

"Come on, Vlad," said Lupus. "Let's go to your room. We need to get some sleep before Auntie Morty wakes us up for the night."

"I should warn you that Master Gory has had a sleepless day," said Mulch. "You'd better have a good excuse for why you are up and about if *he* catches you."

"Okaay," said Vlad shakily.

"Chill, Vlad!" said Lupus. "If Grandpa Gory spots us, I'll think of something."

Vlad shot him a doubtful look.

"It'll be fine!" Lupus said. "Trust me. Thanks for the snacks!" he added, grinning at Mulch.

The butler smiled back. "Thank you, young sir," he said.

The cousins left. They made their way to the East Wing, creeping along as quietly as they could. They were approaching the door to Vlad's room when Grandpa Gory appeared on the landing with Flit and Claw hovering by his side. Vlad was surprised to see that the two creatures were not fighting. He didn't have time to dwell on this, however, as Grandpa's next question threw him into a panic.

"Where have you little devils been?" Gory asked gruffly. "I came to check on you, and you weren't in your coffins!"

"I did try to explain—" Flit began nervously.

"So did I!" squawked Claw.

Flit nodded. "She did!"

"We went to sc—" Lupus said, talking over the creatures.

Vlad gasped. "NO!" he cried.

Lupus carried on "—ooter and skateboard practice in the graveyard," he said. "It's all part of my plan to improve Vlad's coordination for his Bat License."

Vlad didn't dare move. Grandpa looked as though he were about to explode with fury. Vlad held his breath while Flit fluttered next to him, his tiny face creased with worry.

"You've been OUTSIDE?" Gory cried.

Flit and Claw began flapping anxiously and whispering to one another.

We're in trouble now... So much for trusting Lupus! Vlad thought.

Lupus stuck his chin in the air. "I thought if Vlad saw what tombstones looked like in the light he wouldn't be so scared in the dark," he said carelessly.

Gory's stern expression softened slightly. "Ah, I see."

Flit landed on Vlad's shoulder with a sigh of relief and the little vampire let out the breath he'd been holding. Maybe it would be OK, after all.

"Still, you know the three vampire Health and Safety Rules, don't you?" Gory went on, shaking his finger at Lupus. "No Sun, No Sun and NO SUN! What would your parents say?"

Vlad stiffened and Flit squeaked nervously.

Lupus rolled his eyes. "You guys are SO old-fashioned, it's not true!" he said.

"OLD?" Gory repeated. "I am only two

hundred and nine."

Lupus laughed. "Mwahahaha! That's pretty old."

Claw flew to Lupus's shoulder and whispered something to him.

Lupus nodded and went on, "In any case, I meant that you have such old *ideas*. Vampires don't get frazzled anymore. I thought everyone knew that."

Grandpa Gory's furry eyebrows shot up his forehead. "Utter nonsense!" he cried. "My friend Vesuvius Glare went out in the sun..." he began.

Lupus wasn't listening. He had stuck out his arms and was rolling up his sleeves, making a show of inspecting his pale skin. "Let's see... Hmm. Not frazzled. Not even singed!" Lupus said in mock surprise.

Then he looked up at Gory.

"There's this amazing stuff called

'sunscreen,' you know. Don't you have it in England?" He put his hands into his cape and brought out a white tube with an orange lid. "Here," he said, handing it to Grandpa. "It's a human invention. Put it on your skin and it protects you from getting burnt."

Claw gave a caw of approval.

Grandpa's face lit up with excitement. "A human invention, you say? Fascinating!" He grabbed the tube. "I wonder if I could write an extra chapter about human inventions for the *Encyclopedia of Curious Creatures*?" he muttered to himself, as he scanned the words on the tube. "Human beings really are most interesting."

"Quick!" Flit squeaked. "Let's go!"

Vlad immediately dragged Lupus into his room. Flit and Claw followed.

"Phew, that was close," said Flit as Vlad slammed the door behind them. "What did you think you were doing, going to school with Vlad?" he asked Lupus crossly. "If it wasn't for Claw, I wouldn't have even known! She came back and told me she'd followed you to the school gates."

"Caw! You could have gotten Vlad into serious trouble!" said the raven. "Flit's been worried sick."

Lupus made a face. "I see you two are best friends all of a sudden," he said.

Flit flew at him. "You have no idea of the danger you've put Vlad in!" he screeched.

"Flit! STOP!" Vlad cried, grabbing him. "It's OK. No one has guessed that we're vampires."

Lupus looked amused. "I don't know why you are so worried about keeping it a secret anyway."

"Why do you THINK?" Flit shrieked.

Vlad looked at Lupus and then said, "In Transylvania humans and vampires get on fine. Lupus says that two of his best friends at school are humans."

Flit sneered. "I don't believe it," he said. "Mortemia and Drax would've mentioned it after their trip."

"They didn't find out," Lupus said quickly. "Mom and Dad know how traditional Vlad's parents are. They didn't want to worry them."

"That's true," said Claw.

Flit still looked doubtful.

"And I don't want to worry *you*, Flit," Lupus added, making his voice warm and reassuring. "Tell you what – if you let me go to school with Vlad again, I promise I will

teach him some awesome flying skills to show off to Auntie M."

"Sounds fair," said Vlad.

"And I'll make sure we get to go camping on Friday night, too," Lupus added.

"*Camping?*" the little bat exclaimed. "You can't do that!"

"It's OK, Flit," said Lupus. "I know what I'm doing."

"All right," said Flit crossly, as he flew up to the rafters. "But Claw will have to keep an eye on you in the daytime."

"Not a bad idea," said Claw, flying up after the bat.

"Thanks, Flit," said Lupus.

Flit gave a grumpy squeak but said no more.

The two vampires crept into their coffins and snuggled down under the covers.

"Thanks for distracting Grandpa, Lupus," said Vlad with a huge yawn. "That sunscreen

should keep him out of the way!"

"No problem," said Lupus. "Glad to help."

Vlad let out a gentle snore in reply.

Lupus looked over at his cousin and gave a small smile. "What are friends for?" he added softly.

Vlad and Lupus managed only a few hours' sleep before Mortemia woke them for their flying lesson. They yawned and rubbed their eyes as she led them outside.

At least it's a full moon tonight, Vlad thought as he looked around the graveyard. *I can see better and it's not as spooky as normal.*

"We're going to do some bat agility before breakfast!" his mother announced.

"Good idea, Auntie Morty," said Lupus politely.

Mortemia gave a thin-lipped smile in

return. "I'd rather you didn't call me that," she said. "My name is Mortemia."

"Oh, sorry, Auntie Morty— I mean, Mortemia," said Lupus. He winked at Vlad.

Vlad hung his head to hide a smile.

"Lupus, you can start by showing Vlad how to do the course," Mortemia was saying. "Once you have changed into a bat, I want you to fly over to the yew tree and reverse around it – *without* bumping into any branches. Then you must perform a loop-the-loop before flying between those two stone angels over there –" She pointed to two statues on either side of a grave. "It's a tight space, but your wings mustn't touch the statues. Then you will weave in and out of those gravestones in a line there –" She indicated a row of stones. "You'll finish by backflipping back to me and landing the right way up."

Thank badness we didn't have breakfast, Vlad

thought. *I feel sick at the thought of doing all that!*

He shot Lupus a despairing look but Lupus just grinned.

It's OK for him, Vlad thought. *He'll do it perfectly and in double-quick time, then I'll follow and crash into everything.*

His shoulders slumped as he watched Lupus turn into a bat in the blink of an eye. POOF! He was off, whizzing to the tree, reversing around it perfectly, cartwheeling into beautiful loops in the air…

I wish I could be as cool as Lupus, Vlad thought. *If only I could use mind control to make myself as quick and clever…*

He tried to relax, as Lupus had told him to, but it was no use. The more he thought about relaxing, the tenser he felt.

"Vladimir!" His mother's voice made him jump. "Stop shilly-shallying and get on with it!"

"You'll be fine, Vlad," said Lupus. "Remember what I said – just chill."

Vlad closed his eyes and thought *B – A – T*. POOF! He was a bat. He flew toward the yew tree, but once he got there, he couldn't think how to reverse.

I've never done this before! he thought. He began to panic. He tried flapping his wings down and then up, instead of up and then down, but it made no difference. Then he tried circling them, but that made them sore. He turned upside down, but that made him feel dizzy. In the end, he had to fly forward around the tree.

"Zero marks for reversing!" Mortemia barked. "Loop-the-loop next."

Vlad threw himself up and tried to flip over into a circle. He managed an arc and was about to swoop around when a loud noise startled him.

"WHOOOO!"

Vlad shrieked and plummeted to the ground.

"Oh, for badness' sake, it's only an owl!" screeched Mortemia. "You should be able to perform a simple loop-the-loop without being put off so easily. Get up and transform."

Vlad thought *Vampire – Land – Air – Down* and changed back into himself. He hung his head in shame.

"You are a disgrace!" Mortemia shouted. "Lupus, you must stay out here all night with Vlad until he shows some signs of improvement."

Vlad was fed up. He wished he could change his mother into a spider again. *If I did it out here she might get eaten by whatever made that horrible spooky noise*, he thought. But he was too exhausted to try mind control.

He watched miserably as his mother stormed back inside Misery Manor.

"What are we going to do?" he said to Lupus. "If she makes us stay out here and practice, how will we ever be able to get away to go camping?"

"Don't worry about that," said Lupus, his face grim with determination. "We'll go

camping all right. Just you see. But for now, we need to work on your flying. I'll go slowly. Just follow in my tracks."

Vlad got up wearily and did as his cousin said.

It's nice of Lupus to help me, but I don't know why I'm bothering, he thought as he flew up into the night sky. *I may as well pack my things for a long stay in the Black Tower right away.*

By the end of the night Vlad had mastered the loop-the-loop. He still couldn't reverse around the tree, though, and he had crashed into the angels so many times he felt battered and bruised all over. And after the flying lessons he had to stay awake to learn his lines for the auditions. He read them by flashlight under the covers while Lupus slept.

The next day at school Vlad was *so* tired he kept nodding off in class. Minxie had to prod him to keep him awake.

At last, it was time for the auditions. The children had been told that they could do anything they liked – perform a poem, some jokes, a sketch from a well-known play or even something they had written themselves.

Miss Lemondrop asked all the children who were auditioning to go into the auditorium. Lupus came, too.

"I'm not going to audition," he said to Vlad, as they took their places in the auditorium. "I might be good at flying, but I can't act."

Vlad felt grateful for that. The last thing he needed was for Lupus to impress the teachers like he had impressed Mortemia.

"Minxie and Vlad, you're up first," Mr. Bendigo said. "There were some very good auditions yesterday after school. So you'd better show me what *you* can do!"

"We have the best routine EVER!" Minxie announced.

Vlad bit his lip. He wished he had her confidence.

"Go on, Vlad," said Lupus, giving him a little push.

Minxie and Vlad got up onto the stage and arranged some chairs to use as props. They were doing the scene in *Hansel and Gretel* where the two children find the witch's gingerbread house. They spaced some chairs out as if they were trees and put some more in a square, pretending they were the house.

Vlad scanned the audience nervously as he put out the chairs. Some of his friends were there. But Boz was there, too! He stuck his tongue out at Vlad and then grinned mischievously.

I hope he doesn't do anything to put me off my lines, Vlad thought.

He made himself concentrate on the routine he and Minxie had made up on the night she had come for the "spooky sleepover."

"Ready when you are!" said Mr. Bendigo.

"Good luck, Vlad!" cried Ravi.

"Yay!" cheered Leisha, clapping her hands.

"Break a leg," said Boz with a sneer.

"What?" Vlad gasped.

"It's what you say in the theater before a show," Mr. Bendigo explained. "It means 'good luck.'"

"Yeah, maybe," Boz muttered.

Miss Lemondrop gave him a stern look. "Settle down, everyone!" she called. "Off you go," she said to Minxie and Vlad.

They began walking around the stage hand in hand.

"Oooh, these woods are dark," said Minxie, looking scared.

“I think we might be lost,” Vlad quivered.

“Look!” Minxie cried, pointing to the chairs arranged in a square. “A house! Let’s ask for directions.”

Then she ran ahead and jumped into the middle of the chairs, pretending to be the witch inside.

“Knock, knock,” said Vlad.

“Who’s there?” said Minxie in a witchy voice.

“Witch,” said Vlad.

“Eh? But *I’m* the witch…” said Minxie, pretending to look confused. Everyone laughed. “Witch who?” she said.

“Witch is the way home?” said Vlad with an exaggerated wink at the audience.

Mr. Bendigo groaned, but he was smiling. The children laughed again and clapped.

Minxie cackled in a witchy voice and said, “You don’t need to go home, children.

Help yourself to sweets!" Then she ran back around and was Gretel again.

"Mmm," she said, pretending to pick things off the walls and eat them. "A house made of gingerbread and sweets! This is cool."

Vlad acted worried. "I don't think we

should eat anything," he said. "What if the house is haunted?"

"What if it is?" said Minxie. "Haunted houses are cool. Hey, where do you find the scariest haunted houses?" she asked.

"I don't know," said Vlad.

"On a *dead*-end street!" cried Minxie.

Vlad laughed his best vampire laugh. "Mwhahaha! Wicked." Then he looked worried again. "But what if the witch is a bad witch?"

"Not all witches are bad," said Minxie. "Some of them are very glamorous. Do you know what witches put in their hair when they go out at night?"

"No," said Vlad. "What do they put in their hair?"

"*Scare* spray!" said Minxie. There was more laughter from the crowd. "And what is a witch's favorite snack?"

"I dread to think," said Vlad. He stood up tall and pretended to be Mulch. "I hope it's not … *little children,*" he said in a deep booming voice, and he pointed at his friends in the audience.

Leisha shrieked in delight.

"Noooo," said Minxie, rolling her eyes. "They like sand-*witches*!"

Vlad could see that the teachers seemed to be enjoying watching the sketch. Mr. Bendigo was scribbling notes on his clipboard and Miss Lemondrop was smiling. The children in the audience were laughing at all the jokes, too.

Lupus caught Vlad's eye and gave him a thumbs-up.

Vlad began to relax.

"Hey, did you hear about the witch who left school?" he said to Minxie.

"No?" said Minxie. "Why was that?"

PHHHHHRRRRRTTT!

Minxie and Vlad jumped and looked at each other in shock.

A loud farting noise had interrupted their joke!

"Goodness!" said Mr. Bendigo. "What did you eat at lunchtime, Vlad?" he said, while trying not to smile. "I think you could at least say 'pardon me,'" he added.

Vlad's normally pale face had turned quite pink. "It wasn't me!" he protested. As he said this, he caught sight of some movement at the side of the stage.

BUUUURRRRRPP!

A burp erupted from somewhere, making the audience laugh so hard that Vlad and Minxie couldn't remember their lines. They stared at each other, speechless.

Vlad was horrified. He tried to find Lupus in the audience. But now Vlad couldn't see

his cousin. He looked this way and that. Surely it wasn't Lupus making these noises?

THBPBPTHBPTHTHTHTH!

Both teachers were looking cross now. "Vlad – that's enough," said Miss Lemondrop. "Your jokes were good, but blowing raspberries and making other rude noises is *not* funny."

"But—" Vlad protested.

Suddenly there was a yell and Boz was catapulted onto the stage from the wings.

"Help! Help!" he yelled. He ran across the stage and jumped into the audience. "I'm being chased by a big black bird!"

Mr. Bendigo leaped to his feet. "Boswell Jones!" he cried. "Stop running this instant."

Boz screeched to a halt and looked at the teacher, his eyes wide with fear. "But I'm telling you – there's a huge black bird there!"

"Boswell," said Miss Lemondrop, coming over. "You know perfectly well there is no such thing. It is very unkind of you to interrupt Vlad and Minxie's audition like this."

"But – but…" For once Boz was lost for words.

"Go and see Mrs. Viola," said Mr. Bendigo. "And tell her what you've done. You'll be lucky to get a part in the play now."

Boz went bright red in the face, but even he could see that there was no point in arguing. "All right, I'm going," he said, and turned and stomped out of the auditorium. But not before he had given Vlad a very nasty glare.

"Now, Vlad and Minxie, as I was saying," said Miss Lemondrop. "I don't think rude noises are a good idea—"

"Actually, miss, it wasn't Vlad making the noises." Lupus was walking across the stage – he had come from the same direction as Boz.

"What are you doing *there*?" Mr. Bendigo asked, frowning. "Anyone not auditioning is supposed to be sitting quietly in the audience."

"I apologize, sir," said Lupus, with a sweeping bow. "I heard some noises backstage so I thought I should go and investigate. I found Boz hiding with this –" and with a flourish he produced a Whoopie cushion. "He was using it to make the rude noises. He wanted to mess up Vlad and Minxie's audition, sir."

A gasp went around the auditorium.

"Well, thank you, Lupus," said Mr. Bendigo, sounding surprised. "Vlad is lucky to have his cousin looking out for him." He turned to Vlad. "I'm sorry," he said. "Would you and Minxie like to continue with your

sketch? I'm sure we'd all like to see how it ends," he said.

The audience cheered. "Yes! Go on!" they cried.

Minxie beamed. "So, what was that about the witch who left school?" she asked Vlad.

Vlad hesitated. Did they really still have a chance? He glanced at Lupus, who was nodding encouragingly.

"Ahem!" Minxie coughed loudly.

Vlad saw the look in his best friend's eye – he couldn't mess this up. Not after all the hard work Minxie had put into the routine. *This is it,* he told himself. *You have to go for it!* Then he drew himself up tall and put on a voice that sounded exactly like his mother.

"The witch dropped out of school because she had forgotten how to SPELL!" he said, with an expression every bit as withering as Mortemia's.

Both teachers stood up and clapped their hands, and the audience joined in.

Minxie's eyes were shining. "Well done!" she said to Vlad, over the noise of the applause. "You were awesome!"

"Thanks. So were you!" said Vlad, blushing.

Vlad, Lupus and Minxie made their way to the bike shed after the auditions.

"I hope Boz *doesn't* get a part," Minxie said grimly. "By the way," she said to Lupus. "What exactly *did* you do to Boz?"

"You had Claw with you, didn't you?" Vlad said.

"Yes," said Lupus, looking awkward. "I know I took a risk calling her. She's gone now. I had to think quickly – I needed to give Boz a big shock—"

"It's all right," said Vlad. "I'm glad you did.

Thank you." He paused, then he asked, "But *why* did you do it?"

Lupus stared at his feet. "I – I guess I don't like Boz. He reminds me of someone," he said.

"Who?" Vlad asked.

Lupus looked up from under his hair. "Just someone at my school," he said. "You're really lucky to have Minxie as a friend, you know."

"Yes," said Vlad, nodding. "And I want to *keep* her as my friend. That's why I have to make sure that human school stays a secret. So you can't bring Claw here again."

"I get that," said Lupus. His mouth twisted. "I wish I had a friend like Minxie."

Vlad looked at his cousin in amazement. "But you said two of your best friends at home were humans," he said.

Lupus shifted uncomfortably. "That might not have been totally true…" he said.

Minxie gasped. "You lied!" she said.

Vlad eyed his cousin suspiciously. "What else have you been lying about?"

Lupus looked horrified. "I haven't lied about anything else!" he protested. He looked pleadingly at Vlad and Minxie. "Honestly – things are different for vampires back home. I *am* allowed to go outside in the light as long as I wear sunscreen. And I don't have to drink blood and I'm allowed to mix with humans." He stopped and hung his head. "But I don't actually have any real friends," he mumbled.

"But everyone here thinks you're so cool," Vlad said. "You're good at everything – you can do amazing human things like tell stories and do tricks on your scooter *and* you can also do all the vampire skills really well, too. I'm useless compared to you."

Lupus shook his head. "Not useless," he said. "You've made friends with a human.

Sure, in Transylvania we *talk* to humans and mix with them a bit. But with you and Minxie it's special – she doesn't even seem to see you as a vampire."

Minxie shrugged. "I guess not. Vlad is Vlad. He's my best friend and that's all that matters to me."

Vlad felt a warm glow spread through him. "You know what," Vlad said to Lupus, "you *have* got a real friend. You've got me. As long as you'll be Minxie's friend, too," he added.

Lupus grinned. "You bet!" he said.

Minxie punched the air in triumph. "Yay and double yay!" she cried. "That means I've got TWO vampire best friends!"

Later that day at Misery Manor, the cousins were safely tucked up in their coffins in Vlad's room.

"It was amazing the way you got rid of Boz today," Vlad said as he snuggled down.

"Oh, Boz is a lot easier to sort out than you realize. He won't be bothering you again," said Lupus confidently.

Vlad doubted that was true. "You'll be going home on Sunday and then I'll have to face Boz on my own – if I don't get locked in the Black Tower by Mother first..."

"You won't!" Lupus said in an exasperated tone. "I tell you what – let's practice some mind control. Then you'll be able to look after yourself easily without me."

Vlad let out a sigh. "I can't do it unless I'm angry – I've already explained," he said.

Lupus sat up in his coffin. "Buddy, you just need to chill!"

"You keep saying that," said Vlad in despair. "I *can't*."

"Listen," said Lupus, fixing Vlad with a serious expression. "When you're onstage you're super relaxed, right?"

"Suppose," Vlad muttered.

"Thought so," said Lupus. "You *look* relaxed. In fact, I reckon it's the only time I've seen you look truly happy."

Vlad raised his eyebrows. "Really?"

"Yeah!" said Lupus. "You're such a worrier most of the time, but when you get up in

front of your friends and do all your crazy voices and tell your jokes, you're amazing. And you know everyone at school thinks that. You and Minxie will get the main parts for sure."

"How do you know?" Vlad asked. "Other people are good, too."

"Badness me," said Lupus, shaking his head. "You need to have more confidence. You always think you are going to be useless. When you're doing your vampire skills you need to make yourself as relaxed as you are when you're onstage! Then you'll be AMAZING at being a vampire!"

Vlad considered this. "So I should pretend I'm acting?"

Lupus nodded eagerly. "Let's try it now." He leaped out of his coffin and pulled on his cape.

Vlad climbed wearily out of his coffin and put on his cape, too.

"Now, imagine you're onstage. How do you prepare?" Lupus asked.

Vlad shrugged. "I don't. I just pretend I'm Grandpa – or Father, or Mother, or Mulch – and I put on their voices and copy the way they move."

"That's it!" Lupus cried, excited. "That's all you have to do – choose which one of them you'd like to be, and then think of how they move and speak and copy them!"

Vlad felt a fizz of excitement. "You really think it can be that easy?" he asked. "I could just copy my father?"

"Let's give it a try!" said Lupus.

So Vlad thought about how Drax held his head high … and how he spoke in his haughty manner … and how when he turned into a bat, he did it in the blink of an eye … and POOF!

"I'm a bat!" Vlad squeaked, soaring up to

the ceiling. "I've never changed that quickly before."

"Wicked!" Lupus cried. "Now don't stop – carry on thinking about Uncle D. and how he flies."

Vlad imagined his father whizzing like an arrow and reversing sharply around bends. He imagined him drawing circles in the sky as he performed loop-the-loops.

Suddenly he was doing it, too! Vlad was leaping and whirling and twirling and speeding around the room. Even the spiders scurried away when they saw him coming.

"Yay!" Vlad cried. "I can do it! I can do it!" He imagined how his father would land – straight as a dart, quick and sure.

Vlad rocketed down from the rafters and landed softly on his coffin, back in his normal vampire form.

"GREAT!" Lupus shouted, jumping up and down. "Let's try mind control next. Now that you've worked out how to relax, everything will be easy. Just you see."

Lupus was right – once Vlad had realized he could just act at being the kind of vampire his parents wanted him to be, he got better and better at everything. Lupus spent every afternoon after school teaching him, and every time Vlad had a lesson with Mortemia she had to grudgingly admit that he was improving.

On Thursday night she called Drax and Grandpa Gory to watch Vlad fly around the graveyard.

"It seems that my plan has worked – you are a simply *wicked* influence on our son, Lupus," Drax said approvingly as he watched Vlad fly upside down between two tombstones. "I think we should give these two little devils the night off on Friday, don't you?" he said to his wife.

Mortemia's eyebrows knotted together in a frown. "Whatever for?"

"They've worked very hard this week," said Drax. "Remember what Dr. Freakenstein says, 'A rest for one night brings back vampire's bite.' Mwhaha! And besides, I would like to have you to myself this Friday," he added, taking his wife's hand and kissing it.

Vlad couldn't believe it! Friday night was the school camping trip – if his mother agreed to him having a night off, it would be easy to sneak out!

"Great idea, Uncle D.," Lupus said. "We'll be all right with Grandpa Gory and Mulch."

Vlad glanced at his cousin. Was he controlling Drax's mind?

"Splendid," said Drax. "Mortemia and I haven't been on a night flight for pleasure in centuries. What do you say, my little blood cell?"

Vlad caught Lupus looking at him encouragingly.

His cousin raised one eyebrow, then mouthed, *Mind control – now you do it!*

Vlad took a deep breath. What would Lupus do…?

He would relax…

…he would focus on Mortemia…

…then he would make her think about how nice a night flight would be…

Suddenly Vlad's mother beamed. "What a devilish idea, Drax! I *could* do with a night off from teaching."

Vlad looked across at his cousin in amazement. He had done it! He had controlled his mother's mind without getting angry – and now he could go on the school camping trip!

At last it was Friday afternoon. Everything had gone according to plan. Not only had Lupus managed to help him impress his parents and get the night off, but his cousin had also successfully used mind control on Grandpa Gory AND Miss Lemondrop! Gory believed that Vlad and Lupus were spending the night studying vampire folklore and "should not be disturbed," and Miss Lemondrop had not once asked for the permission letter from Vlad's parents.

"We're free!" Lupus shouted, as he and

Vlad found their seats on the school bus that afternoon.

They got to the campsite late in the day. The bus dropped the children and teachers in the parking lot and everyone walked a little way into the woods with Miss Lemondrop in front and Mr. Bendigo bringing up the rear.

"This is the perfect spot," said Miss Lemondrop as they came to a clearing. "Mr. Bendigo and I will put up the tents. And children, you can make a start gathering firewood, then we'll have some activities."

There were lots of broken twigs and small branches on the ground. The children chattered excitedly as they picked up armfuls of wood. Soon there was a heap of it in the middle of the clearing.

The only child not joining in was Boz. He was watching Lupus very carefully. As Vlad and Minxie added some wood to the pile,

Boz approached them.

"You should stay away from him," he said, pointing at Lupus. "He's weird. Even weirder than you," he added, sneering at Vlad. "He did something at school the other day – I know it was him that set that bird on me."

Minxie rolled her eyes. "Everyone knows you're lying, Boz," she said. "No one else saw a bird."

Boz snarled and opened his mouth to say something in return, but Mr. Bendigo interrupted.

"Boswell, will you help me find some leaves and pine cones, please?"

Boz muttered something under his breath, but he followed the teacher and left Vlad and Minxie with the others.

Miss Lemondrop was getting some cushions out of a bag. She asked Minxie to help her put them around in a circle.

"Everyone find a cushion and sit down," she said to the class, "and I will tell you what we are going to do."

The children scurried to their places and sat cross-legged in a circle.

"First, we are going on a short nature walk to gather decorations for our nature crowns," said the teacher. "And we'll look out for minibeasts such as worms and

beetles and spiders."

Leisha gasped and jumped up, looking around her fearfully.

"What's the matter, Leisha?" asked Miss Lemondrop.

"I don't like spiders," she said.

Vlad shuffled a little closer to Minxie. He didn't like them either.

Minxie took his hand and gave it a squeeze. "It'll be all right," she whispered.

"There's nothing to worry about, Leisha," Miss Lemondrop said. "We're only going to observe the minibeasts. We don't suggest anyone touches any creatures – they are more frightened of us than we are of them. It won't be a long walk, anyway," she added. "It'll soon be dark."

Dark? Spiders? Poor Vlad gulped. This camping trip was not turning out to be as lovely as he had hoped it would be!

"Later on, we'll cook some sausages over the campfire and toast some marshmallows," the teacher went on. She smiled at Vlad as she spoke. He tried to remember to relax, as Lupus was always telling him to do. "Then we'll listen to the music that nature makes – the sounds of the night creatures and the wind in the trees."

The nature walk was fun in the end. Even the minibeasts weren't that scary. They were much smaller than the spiders in Misery Manor and they all scuttled away when the children got near. Vlad stuck close to Minxie just in case. She was much braver about creepy-crawlies than he was.

The best bit was making the nature crowns with the beautiful leaves and berries and nuts and cones that the children had found.

Afterward, the teachers showed them how to light a campfire safely. Then they asked the children to sit quietly, wearing their crowns.

"Listen to the sounds of the woodland," said Miss Lemondrop.

"WHOOOO!"

Vlad jumped. It was the same noise as he'd heard in the graveyard the other night!

"It's only an owl," said Mr. Bendigo.

"EEEEEK!"

Vlad jumped again.

"Another owl," said Mr. Bendigo. "Probably a female tawny owl – they make a screeching noise and the male answers with a softer sound. People describe it as one sound – 'Too-whit, too-whoo!' – but it's actually two owls talking to one another."

Vlad's fluttering heart calmed a little. *I'm being silly,* he told himself. *Lupus is right. There's nothing to worry about.*

But he didn't like looking out into the blackness beyond the campfire. And he couldn't help thinking about the spiders now that it was dark. What if they crawled into his tent?

Mr. Bendigo could see that Vlad was still afraid. "Let's talk about how the dark makes us feel," he said.

Scared, Vlad thought.

"There's nothing as frightening as your

own imagination!" said Ravi boldly. "That's what my gran says."

"Yeah, Boz would know all about imagining things," said Lupus with a wink.

"I didn't imagine anything," Boz snapped. "You made a big bird appear from nowhere!"

"That's enough, Boswell," said Miss Lemondrop sternly.

"There's no such thing as total darkness anyway," said Ravi. "Look, there are stars and there's the moon." He pointed to the inky-dark sky, which was filled with dazzling stars.

"That's right," said Miss Lemondrop, smiling. "Now, let's cook our supper."

Vlad relaxed as the sausages sizzled over the fire. The delicious smell filled his nostrils and made his tummy rumble. *Humans have a much better life than vampires*, he thought.

Soon the sausages had been eaten, the marshmallows toasted, and everyone was

lounging on their cushions, feeling full and content.

"I've got an idea – how about a story around the campfire before bed?" said Lupus.

Mr. Bendigo beamed. "I think we'd all like that."

Miss Lemondrop nodded. "As long as it's not a scary one," she added.

Lupus made a face. "But those are the best ones!" he said.

"Yeah!" Ravi cried. "You've got to have a good ghost story around the campfire!"

"Yes!" everyone agreed.

Vlad wasn't so sure. He had only just gotten used to sitting out in the dark.

"Don't worry," Lupus whispered, nudging him. "It has a funny ending."

"All right," said Vlad reluctantly.

"Go on then, Lupus," said Mr. Bendigo.

Lupus cleared his throat and began speaking

in a low and spooky voice. "One night a girl was walking through the woods on her own when she heard a BUMP BUMP BUMP behind her." He banged his foot against the ground to make the bumping sound.

Minxie and some of the others squealed in delight.

"She started walking faster, but the BUMP BUMP BUMP continued…" Lupus went on, banging his foot again. "The girl couldn't resist sneaking a peek to see what it was that was following her…"

"What was it?" Leisha asked, hiding behind her hands.

"A COFFIN!" Lupus cried, leaping up.

A gasp went around the campfire.

"The girl screamed – ARGH!" Lupus let out a blood-curdling shriek, and all the children joined in, giggling and screaming.

Lupus began prowling around the circle.

"The girl ran as fast as she could." Lupus stared into everyone's eyes. "But to her horror, the coffin chased her, BUMP BUMP BUMP faster and faster..."

Everyone was squealing now.

"The girl ran all the way out of the woods, back to her house. She sprinted up the path and up the steps to her door. She struggled to get her key in the lock, and all the time the coffin was chasing her – BUMP BUMP BUMP!"

Lupus paused dramatically.

"What happened next?" cried Ravi.

"Finally," said Lupus, "the girl managed to get inside and lock the door behind her."

"Phew!" said Minxie.

"Bah. That's a rubbish story," said Boz.

"BUT!" cried Lupus, raising one finger. "The coffin came crashing through the front door and chased her up the staircase!"

Ravi screamed and pulled the hood of his sweatshirt down over his face.

"She ran upstairs and shut herself in the bathroom," Lupus went on. "The girl was totally exhausted now. She slid down against the bathtub and sat, puffing and panting, hoping that she was safe... Then the coffin smashed through the bathroom door as well – she was trapped!"

At this, Leisha shrieked and leaped onto Miss Lemondrop's lap!

"She was brave, though, this girl, and determined to survive," said Lupus. "She looked around the room for anything she could find to save herself. She grabbed the nearest thing—"

"A can of hair spray to spray it with!" shouted Ravi.

"Some toilet cleaner to throw at it!" cried Leisha.

"No!" said Lupus. "She took a bottle of cold medicine from the cabinet…"

"This story is terrible," Boz grumbled.

Lupus ignored him. "Desperate now, the girl hurled the medicine at the coffin and…"

He paused again and looked around at his audience.

"AND WHAT?" everyone shouted.

"And the *coffin stopped*!" Lupus cried. "Get it? Cold medicine? The 'coffin' – the coughing – stopped? Mwhahahaha!"

A loud groan went around the campfire, followed by laughter and a big round of applause.

"Thank you, thank you," said Lupus, taking a bow.

Vlad and Minxie cheered and clapped louder than anyone.

Only Boz did not join in. He sat, staring at the flames and sulking.

"Very entertaining," said Mr. Bendigo. "Acting skills clearly run in the family."

"Yeah, like freaky teeth and a weird laugh," Boz mumbled.

But no one was listening to him.

Lupus found his seat next to Vlad.

"That was awesome!" Vlad said. "I wish you didn't have to go home on Sunday."

"Yeah!" said Minxie. "I wish you were staying longer, too."

Lupus looked sad. "I don't want to go," he

said. "But I think your mom'll say you don't need me anymore, Vlad."

"What do you mean?" Vlad asked.

Lupus counted off on his fingers. "Your flying's improved, your mind control is getting better – and you're out in the dark, having fun!" he said.

Vlad gasped as he realized what this meant. "Yes – I'm not afraid anymore!" he said.

Minxie and Lupus cheered.

Lupus and Vlad were exhausted by the time they got back to Misery Manor on Saturday at lunchtime. They raced straight to their coffins to catch up on some rest.

It seemed as though they had been asleep for only a matter of minutes when Mortemia came into the room and shook them awake.

"I would've thought you'd be up dark and early tonight," she said crossly as the two vampires groaned, stretched and yawned.

"But it's Saturday!" said Lupus.

Mortemia arched one perfectly plucked

eyebrow. "What's that got to do with anything?" she asked.

Lupus let out a disbelieving laugh. "Don't you ever sleep in?" he asked.

Mortemia's nostrils flared with disgust. It seemed she had suddenly had enough of trying to be polite to her husband's nephew.

"I know you Transylvanian vampires have modern ideas, but *sleeping in* is taking things too far." She sniffed. "That kind of lazy nonsense will get you nowhere, young vampire. It's a good job you're leaving tomorrow."

Vlad sat up and blinked as his mother pulled back the covers on his coffin.

"I hope you're ready for the Bat License test, Vladimir," she said. "If you pass you will not have to have flying lessons ever again."

"And – if I fail?" Vlad asked, his voice small.

"You know what happens if you fail," said

Mortemia. "You will go to the Black Tower. If it had been up to me you would've been sent there a long time ago to think about your behavior. But your father seems convinced that you will learn better by following Lupus's example. We have yet to see who is right," she sneered.

Vlad shot Lupus a look of desperation.

Lupus made a face and hopped out of his coffin. "Vlad will pass, don't worry," he said. "He's had the best teacher – me!"

"Little show-off," Mortemia grumbled. "Out you go – into the graveyard for the test!"

At least I've conquered my fear of the dark, Vlad thought as he followed his mother. He knew now that the shadowy shapes he had been so frightened of were trees and bushes and tombstones. And he knew from the camping trip that the ghostly noises were little

creatures like owls.

As for my maneuvers, Vlad thought, *I must just "chill," like Lupus told me, and pretend I'm onstage. If I act like Lupus I might be OK.*

Drax and Grandpa Gory were waiting in the graveyard. Drax had his pocket watch at the ready to time Vlad's circuit. Grandpa had some parchment and a quill to take notes on Vlad's performance.

"Don't forget the checklist, Gory," said Mortemia as she swept past to take her place next to him. "Every one of those maneuvers must be completed to perfection for Vlad to get his license."

"There's no need to tell me," said Gory. "It's like teaching an old vampire how to suck blood," he added irritably.

Vlad glanced over at his grandfather. Gory

rolled his eyes and nodded to Mortemia as if to say, "What a pain!"

Vlad smiled gratefully. *At least there's a chance that Grandpa will be fair,* he thought.

Lupus was already a bat, looping and twirling and showing off as he zipped in between the tombstones. "Just remember what I taught you, Vlad!" he squeaked.

"Stop it!" Mortemia snapped. "This is Vlad's test, not yours."

"Calm down, my little blood cell," said Drax smoothly. He took Mortemia's bony hand. "Why don't you read out the list of skills that Vlad has to complete? Then we'll get this over and done with, and go inside for a celebratory breakfast."

Mortemia snorted. "Very well." She drew out a piece of parchment from inside her cape. "First the safety checks," she said, reading from the list.

Bat License Test
Safety checks
Morphing in and out of bat form
Takeoff and landing
Night vision – can you read
a tombstone 60 feet away?
Long-distance flying –
safety measures, rest times, etc.
Moving out into oncoming traffic
Turning right
Reversing
Flying between buildings /
through a narrow space
Flying upside down

Vlad pictured his cousin changing into a bat. He did it so fast! Vlad closed his eyes and imagined he was as skilled as Lupus. And POOF! He was a bat – as easy as that!

Vlad immediately felt happier. He flew in front of his mother. "Wings – check," he said, flapping them up and down. "Night vision – check," he said, looking around. "Hearing – check," he finished, flicking his ears. He was still amazed at how much better his hearing was when he was a bat.

"Very good!" said Gory, making checks on his parchment.

"Hmm," said Mortemia. "Let's test that night vision. Read that tombstone over there."

Vlad peered at the stone, which was on the other side of the graveyard. "OK – 'in loving memory of Bertie Hill,'" he said. "'1902–1967. May he rest in peace.'"

"Wicked!" shouted Drax. "Your night vision has improved no end, son."

Lupus smiled encouragingly at Vlad.

Mortemia pursed her lips. "All right," she said. "And now for the flying skills."

Vlad took another deep breath. *Just remember to act like Lupus, and everything will be OK,* he said to himself.

And it was! In the next half an hour, Vlad zipped in and out of the tombstones with speed and elegance, not bumping into a single one. Then he reached the yew tree and did a perfect reverse maneuver. Next, he flew back to his mother upside down.

Drax and Gory and Lupus were clapping and cheering in delight.

"You've done it!" cried Drax. "At last I think we can say you are a real vampire."

"Wait a minute," said Mortemia, tapping one bloodred nail against her list. "What

about pulling out into oncoming traffic?"

Drax put his head on one side. "Oh, my little devil," he said. "I don't think that's strictly necessary, is it? There isn't much traffic around here, after all."

Gory agreed. "No vampire traffic other than us, and we rarely leave the manor these days."

"That's *not* the point!" Mortemia insisted. "We had to do it to get our licenses, so Vlad must, too."

"B-but I haven't practiced that!" Vlad squeaked.

"Too bad," said his mother, turning into a bat. "Come on, Gory – and Drax. You too, Lupus. You fly around in the middle of the graveyard with me. Vlad – you must decide when it's safe to cross the graveyard, making sure you don't bump into any of us."

Vlad swallowed. He didn't know the

rules! Should he nip out as fast as possible and dodge his relatives? Or should he wait until there was a big enough gap and cross slowly? He wanted to shout, "IT'S NOT FAIR!" but he knew he just had to do as he was told.

Lupus flew up to him and whispered quickly. "Relax, remember?"

It was all very well him giving advice like that, Vlad thought, but his nerves were beginning to get the better of him. It was hard to stay relaxed!

Mortemia, Drax, Gory and Lupus began flying around the middle of the graveyard. At first they were tightly packed together. Then they started separating and flying in different directions. Suddenly, Vlad saw a gap big enough to fly through. He gathered all his courage and took aim at the gap, flying in a neat straight line.

Just as he was about to go through, his mother turned sharply and flew toward him.

"Argh!" he cried. His wings wouldn't do what he wanted them to. "Help!" he shouted, as the bat shape of his mother approached, faster and faster.

They were going to crash!

Vlad closed his eyes and waited for the collision. He felt a rush of air and heard a screech from his mother.

Then, without thinking, he flipped up and back and performed a backward somersault, narrowly missing his mother by an inch.

Mortemia had not been expecting this and kept flying straight – heading directly for the yew tree!

"I can't STOP!" she yelled. She crashed into the branches and plummeted to the ground, landing in a crumpled heap.

Drax, Gory and Lupus pinged back into

vampire form and walked over to her. Vlad hovered above them, not daring to transform himself. What would his mother do now? She was bound to punish him for causing her to crash.

"Mortemia?" said Drax, his forehead crinkled into a frown. "Are you all right?"

Mortemia pinged back into vampire form and stood up, rubbing her head crossly. "No, I am not!" she snapped. "Did you see what our useless son just did?"

"Erm, yes. I did," said Drax slowly. "Although I wouldn't call him 'useless.'"

"Why not?" Mortemia cried. "He made me CRASH!"

Drax picked up the parchment that had dropped from Mortemia's cape. "Actually," he said, "I think you'll find that Vlad performed a wonderfully elegant maneuver to *avoid* crashing into you – and *you* were the

one that crashed."

Grandpa nodded. "That is true," he said. "Vlad used some very quick thinking there. You were flying rather recklessly, if you ask me."

"I *didn't* ask you!" Mortemia screeched. "Vlad, you know what this means—" she began, shaking her finger at Vlad.

"It means that Vlad has passed his Bat License!" said Lupus, coming to Vlad's rescue. "Come on, Vlad. Change back and join us down here."

Vlad hesitated.

Then, all at once, his mother gave in.

"All right," said Mortemia irritably. "I can see I have been outvoted."

Grandpa Gory, Drax and Lupus all cheered.

Vlad was delighted! He changed back into a vampire almost without thinking. POOF!

And he landed softly next to his mother, holding his head high.

"I'm sorry you hurt your head," he said politely. "But you were going really fast."

"Yes, yes," said Mortemia. "You'd better take this quickly, before I change my mind," she said, reaching into her cape. Then she shoved a piece of parchment at Vlad and stormed back into Misery Manor, muttering angrily to herself.

"Wow," said Vlad, his eyes wide as he read the document. "Fully Fledged Bat License – valid for one hundred years."

"Congratulations, Vlad!" said Drax, slapping his son on the back.

"Good work!" said Grandpa Gory.

"Yeah, well done," said Lupus. "You'll be able to come and visit me now."

"I think I'd actually like that," said Vlad.

"And I'll make sure MY mom doesn't cause a traffic accident when you do!" Lupus added.

Drax and Grandpa exchanged an amused glance.

Then the vampires threw back their heads and gave a long, hearty laugh. "Mwhahahaha!"

"Thank you, Lupus," said Vlad. "For everything," he added quietly.

"No problem, buddy," said Lupus. "Now – race you back inside!" he cried, pinging back into bat form.

"You bet!" Vlad shouted, transforming in an instant.

"Fang-tastic," said Drax softly, as he watched his son speed off into the night. "A real vampire at last."

Anna Wilson LOVES stories. She has been a bookworm since she could first hold a book and always knew she wanted a job that involved writing or reading or both. She has written picture books, short stories, poems and young fiction series. Anna lives with her family in Bradford-on-Avon, Wiltshire, England.

www.annawilson.co.uk

Kathryn has a passion for illustration, design, animation, film and puppetry! She attended Sheridan College for the Bachelor of Applied Arts – 2D Animation Program and completed an internship at Pixar Animation Studios for storyboarding. She loves working on children's entertainment, publications and media – especially kids' books – and television series. She is currently based in Toronto, Canada.

www.kathryndurst.com

READ THEM ALL!

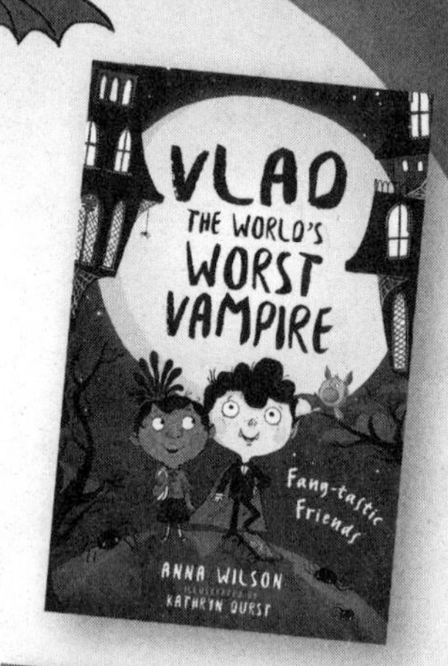